gust, 9, 2014

Camellia!

...on the beginning of our adventure

Love,
Aleksandra

Minnie and the Lost Dog

This edition published by Parragon Inc. in 2013

Parragon Inc.
440 Park Avenue South, 13th Floor
New York, NY 10016
www.parragon.com

ISBN 978-1-4723-2721-5

Printed in China

Minnie and the Lost Dog

Bath • New York • Singapore • Hong Kong • Cologne • Delhi
Melbourne • Amsterdam • Johannesburg • Shenzhen

"Minnie!" cried Mickey Mouse over the phone. "I need your help!"

"What's the matter, Mickey?" Minnie Mouse asked.

"I have to be in town in ten minutes for a dentist's appointment, and Goofy promised to play with Pluto while I'm gone. But he hasn't shown up yet, and Pluto is begging for a walk in the park. Can you come over?"

"I'll be there in a jiffy," Minnie promised as she pulled on her coat.

Minnie and Pluto were playing ball in the park when Daisy Duck arrived.

"Want to come shopping with me?" Daisy asked Minnie. "There's a super new shoe store on Poteet Street."

"Sorry, but I can't," said Minnie. "I promised Mickey I'd look after Pluto while he's at the dentist. He'll be away at least another half hour."

Daisy smiled. "That's not very long," she said. "I'll wait with you until he gets home." So the friends headed back to Mickey's house.

Suddenly, Minnie and Daisy heard a shriek coming from outside. "Help!" cried a neighbor. "My cat is stuck in a tree!"

Before Minnie or Daisy could reply, the neighbor started dragging them away. "Wait," Minnie cried. "What about Pluto?"

"You mean that dog?" said the neighbor. "He can't come—poor Pussykins will be so terrified that she'll never come down!"

Minnie hesitated. But the neighbor needed them. "We'll be right back," Minnie promised as she tied Pluto's leash to the trunk of a shady tree. She tested the knot, making sure it was tight enough.

It took only a few minutes to coax Pussykins down from her perch in the tree. But when Minnie and Daisy got back to Mickey's yard, they were met with a dreadful surprise. Pluto was gone!

"But how?" Minnie cried. "He couldn't have unhooked the leash by himself."

Daisy grabbed her friend's arm. "Do you know what this means, Minnie?" she said with a gulp. "Pluto has been dognapped!"

Minnie and Daisy searched the rest of the yard, then hurried up and down the street, questioning everyone they met.

"I just passed a dog," said an elderly man. "He was with a short, stout, grumpy-looking fellow in a red hat."

"It must have been Pluto!" Minnie cried. "Which way did they go?"

The man pointed. "Over that way," he said.

Minnie and Daisy raced down the street. They almost ran right past a man in a red hat, walking a bulldog.

"Daisy, wait," Minnie said, stopping to look again. The man was short and stout. He also looked pretty grumpy, grunting and groaning as he tried to get his dog to move.

The man saw Minnie staring at his dog. "He's lazier than mud," he snapped, sounding as grumpy as he looked. "If I didn't drag him out for a walk twice a day, he'd never move a muscle."

"That must be the dog that the old man was talking about," Minnie said to Daisy as the man in the red hat dragged his bulldog away.

"But that's not Pluto!" Daisy cried. "Oh, I get it," she said a moment later. "We forgot to describe him. We forgot to say that he's a golden-brown dog."

"Did you say you're looking for a golden-brown dog?" asked a little girl as she tugged on Minnie's sleeve. "I just saw one. He's tied to the mailbox across from the park."

"Thanks a bunch!" said Minnie.

She and Daisy ran toward the park. "This time it's got to be Pluto," Daisy cried. "How many golden-brown dogs could there be around here?"

Daisy and Minnie turned the corner and saw the mailbox.

Minnie stopped short. "I think I know the answer to that," she said. "There are at least two golden-brown dogs around here."

A dog was tied to the postbox. He had golden-brown fur—but he wasn't Pluto.

"Oh, no!" Daisy cried. "Will we ever find him?"

Minnie asked a passing mailman if he had seen any dogs.

"I saw a poodle with sharp teeth in the yard on the corner," the mailman said. "I barely escaped with my pants in one piece. Besides that, I saw only one other dog. A tall, gangly fellow was walking him."

"Was the dog about this high, with golden-brown fur and a green collar?" Daisy asked, raising her hand to Pluto's height.

The mailman nodded. "That's right. The guy walking him had a big nose and big feet, and he was carrying a purple ball."

"A purple ball!" Daisy exclaimed. "The dognapper not only dognapped Pluto—he stole his toy, too!"

Minnie nodded thoughtfully. "Which way were they walking?" she asked.

"That way," the letter carrier said, pointing toward the park.

Minnie turned to Daisy. "I think I know who took Pluto," she said. "Come on, let's go!"

Daisy followed Minnie into the park. Sure enough, they soon spotted Pluto, safe and sound. And standing right next to him was—Goofy!

"So, I was right!" said Minnie. "Goofy was the dognapper."

Goofy scratched his head and looked bewildered. "Dognapper?" he asked.

"We thought someone had stolen Pluto from Mickey's yard," Minnie said as she gave Pluto a big hug.

"Gawrsh," Goofy said. "Sorry about that. When I saw my little pal tied to that tree, I figured Mickey left him there to wait for me. I promised to look after him, but my watch broke so I was a little late."

"How did you figure out that Pluto was with Goofy?" Daisy asked Minnie.

"I knew a dognapper wouldn't take the ball," Minnie said. "But a dog walker would. And when the mailman pointed to the park, I knew I had solved the mystery."

"I get it!" said Daisy. Goofy nodded.

Pluto barked happily and Minnie laughed. "I guess that's Pluto's way of saying that three dog walkers are better than one."

Daisy nodded. "And definitely better than one dognapper!"